COOKING with BEAR

A Story and Recipes from the Forest

PICTURES BY

Deborah Hodge   *Lisa Cinar*

GROUNDWOOD BOOKS

HOUSE OF ANANSI PRESS

TORONTO   BERKELEY

Text copyright © 2019 by Deborah Hodge
Illustrations copyright © 2019 by Lisa Cinar
Published in Canada and the USA in 2019 by Groundwood Books

Groundwood Books / House of Anansi Press
groundwoodbooks.com

We gratefully acknowledge for their financial support of our publishing program the Canada Council for the Arts, the Ontario Arts Council and the Government of Canada.

Canada Council for the Arts   Conseil des Arts du Canada

ONTARIO ARTS COUNCIL
CONSEIL DES ARTS DE L'ONTARIO
an Ontario government agency
un organisme du gouvernement de l'Ontario

With the participation of the Government of Canada
Avec la participation du gouvernement du Canada | Canadä

Library and Archives Canada Cataloguing in Publication
Hodge, Deborah, author
Cooking with Bear / Deborah Hodge ; pictures by Lisa Cinar.
Includes recipes.
Issued in print and electronic formats.
ISBN 978-1-77306-074-3 (hardcover). — ISBN 978-1-77306-075-0 (PDF)
I. Cinar, Lisa, illustrator II. Title.
PS8565.O295C66 2019   jC813'.6   C2018-902675-8
C2018-902676-6

The illustrations in this book were created with a combination of ink, watercolor, Photoshop and a dash of forest magic.
Design by Michael Solomon and Sara Loos
Printed and bound in Malaysia

MIX
Paper from responsible sources
FSC
www.fsc.org FSC® C012700

In memory of Sheila Barry, who made the world a brighter, better place. — DH

For Brandy, Christy and Sue for helping me cook up all sorts of things . . . mostly ideas! Und für meine gute Freundin Veronika mit der ich glücklicherweise die härtesten "Plätzchen" der Welt backen konnte! — LC

AUTHOR'S ACKNOWLEDGMENTS
Thank you to Emma Sakamoto and all the Groundwood recipe testers and tasters. Your help was invaluable! Love and thanks to Emily Garner, Helen Hodge and Katherine Garner for delicious recipes and advice; to Molly, Xavier, Jack and Finn, fine young chefs and fun kitchen companions; and to my wonderful family, some of the best cooks I know.

PUBLISHER'S NOTE
Neither the Publisher nor the Author shall be liable for any damage or injury that may be caused or sustained as a result of conducting any of the activities in this book without specifically following instructions, conducting the activities without proper supervision or ignoring the cautions contained in the book. All children need to work with adult guidance and supervision, and it is the parent or guardian's responsibility to ensure that the child is working safely. Babies under a year should not be given honey. Please be advised that some of the recipes contain nuts.

Author's Note

In this story, Bear collects and cooks with many delicious foods that grow in and around his forest. He shares his favorite recipes with you, too.

Bear looks in the forest for foods that are ripe and ready in each season. Since you are not a bear, you can look at your local grocery store or farmer's market for foods that are in season and grown near your home. Or if you are really keen, you can plant a garden.

Bear gathers wild greens, herbs, fruits, nuts and seeds for his recipes. You can look for the same kinds of "non-wild" ingredients (such as apples, berries, watercress, arugula, hazelnuts, sunflower seeds and honey) grown by local farmers and sold at your market. Please use them to make the recipes in this book.

If you would like to learn to forage for wild foods, ask your parents to look for courses offered by foraging experts who know how to correctly identify edible plants of the forest.

Bear and I want you to always cook with an adult, and ask for their help with anything sharp or hot. Be safe, and most of all, have fun!

Happy cooking!

Deborah (and Bear)

IT HAD BEEN a long, cold winter in the forest. Bear looked out his window and saw bright sun and the snow beginning to melt.

"Spring is late this year," he said.

Bear was cozy inside his den, but he wondered about his friends. Were they warm? Did they have enough to eat?

"I will check on them today," he said.

But first, he had some cooking to do.

Watercress Soup

Bear combines fresh watercress and potatoes to make a tasty spring soup.

1 tbsp olive oil

½ large sweet onion, roughly chopped (about 1 cup)

1 clove garlic, minced

1 large russet potato, peeled and roughly chopped (about 1 cup)

1 tbsp butter

pinch of salt and pepper

1¾ cups chicken or vegetable stock

large bunch of watercress

drizzle of cream (optional)

With an adult's help, heat the oil over medium heat in a large saucepan. Add the onions and garlic and fry them, stirring often, until the onions are soft and golden (about 5 to 7 minutes).

Add the potatoes and butter to the pan. Toss the potatoes with the onion mixture and fry for a minute or two until the potatoes are coated with butter. Sprinkle with salt and pepper.

Add the stock and simmer for about 15 minutes or until the potatoes are soft.

Rinse the watercress and shake off the excess water. Then remove the large stems and roughly chop the leaves. (You should be left with about 1 cup of leaves.) Add them to the soup and cook for 2 to 3 minutes more, until the leaves are slightly wilted.

With an adult's help, purée the soup with a hand blender until it is smooth. (Alternatively, use a potato masher, being careful to avoid splashing.) Small pieces of bright green watercress will remain.

Taste, and add salt and pepper as needed.

Ladle the soup into bowls and drizzle with a little cream if desired.

Makes 2 large bowls or 4 small ones.

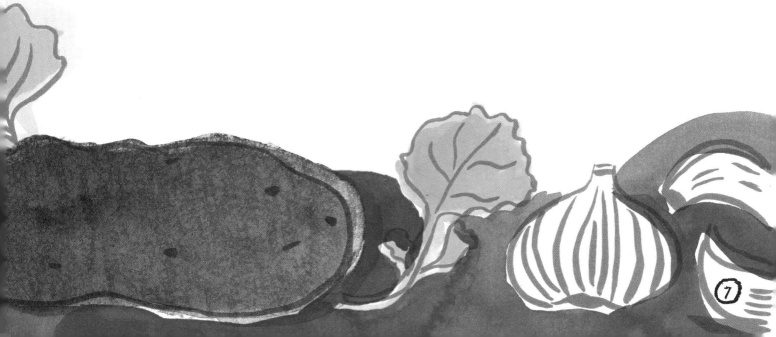

When the soup was simmering, Bear heard a knock at his door.

"Fox!" he said. "I'm so glad to see you!"

"I smelled something yummy," said Fox. "I knew you were awake."

"I couldn't sleep anymore," said Bear. "I'm ready for spring. Would you like to join me for lunch?"

"Oh, yes!" said Fox. "I'm so tired of eating the same old thing. I'd love to try something new."

Bear served up steaming bowls of watercress soup with slices of crusty seed bread and wild herb butter. Then came dessert — warm maple-apple crisp topped with a scoop of honey ice cream.

Fox gobbled up his meal.

"Wow!" he said. "Can you teach me to cook like this?"

"I'd be glad to," said Bear. "The forest is full of delightful things to eat. Let's go for a walk and I'll show you where I gather my food. We can visit our friends, too."

"Hello, Squirrel," called Bear. "Fox and I are wondering how you are after the long, cold winter, and if you've had enough to eat?"

"I'm fine," said Squirrel. "I stored a lot of nuts before the snow came and I have a few left. Would you like some?"

"Yes, please," said Bear. "I'm giving Fox cooking lessons. I'll show him how to make my favorite nut dishes."

Nut Burgers

Squirrel is always happy to eat Bear's nut burgers. She likes hers mini-sized!

⅓ cup ground hazelnuts*

⅓ cup ground peanuts*

⅔ cup bread crumbs

⅓ cup grated aged cheddar cheese

2 to 3 tsp finely chopped fresh herbs (basil and parsley are tasty)

1 tbsp vegetable oil to make the burgers (plus a little more for frying them)

½ cup finely chopped onions

1 clove garlic, minced

⅓ cup finely chopped mushrooms

½ cup grated carrots (using medium to large-sized holes on a grater)

1 tbsp butter

2 eggs, lightly beaten

pinch of salt and pepper

In a mixing bowl, stir together the nuts, bread crumbs, cheese and herbs. Set aside.

With an adult's help, heat the oil in a frying pan over medium heat. Add the onions and garlic and fry them until the onions are soft and golden (about 5 to 7 minutes). Add the mushrooms, carrots and butter and fry until the mushrooms are soft (about 2 to 3 minutes). Remove from heat.

Add the vegetables to the nut mixture, then add the eggs and salt and pepper. Stir until well blended and the mixture forms a ball.

With your hands, form the mixture into burger patties (not too thin). You can make 4 regular-sized patties or 8 mini patties (slider-sized).

Ask an adult to help you fry the patties in a lightly greased pan over medium heat, turning once, until they are golden brown and crispy on both sides.

Serve the patties on burger buns (regular or slider-sized) with your favorite burger toppings, such as lettuce and tomatoes. Or eat in a pita with yogurt and sliced cucumbers, or on top of your spring greens salad (page 26).

MAKES 4 REGULAR-SIZED OR 8 MINI-SIZED BURGERS.

*Ask an adult to help you grind the nuts in a blender or food processor, pulsing for a few seconds at a time until they are a fine and even grind. (You can easily adapt this recipe and substitute other kinds of nuts, cheese or herbs as desired.)

Bear and Fox waved to Chickadee in her home at the top of the tallest tree.

"Chickadee! How are you faring?" called Bear.

"I'm well," she said. "I puffed up my feathers like a warm sleeping bag and stayed very snug all winter long."

"We'd like to know what you've been eating," said Bear. "Fox is trying to spice up his diet."

"I've got extra berries and seeds that I dried last summer," said Chickadee. "May I share some with you?"

"Thank you," said Bear. "Fox and I will make honey-roasted granola. These will be a perfect addition."

Honey-Roasted Granola

You can make granola with any combination of nuts, seeds and dried fruit. This recipe uses Bear's favorite mix of ingredients.

1 cup rolled oats

¾ cup chopped nuts (such as almonds and pecans)

⅓ cup seeds (such as green pumpkin seeds/pepitas and sunflower seeds)

⅓ cup unsweetened shredded coconut

pinch of salt

¾ cup dried fruit (such as raisins and dried cranberries)

HONEY MIXTURE

3 tbsp honey (warmed slightly — about 5 seconds in the microwave)

3 tbsp canola oil

1 tsp vanilla

with Dried Cranberries

Preheat the oven to 325°F. Line a rimmed baking sheet with parchment paper.

In a mixing bowl, stir together the oats, nuts, seeds, coconut and salt.

In a small bowl, combine the honey, oil and vanilla.

Pour the honey mixture over the oat mixture and toss until the oats are well coated.

Spread the granola mixture across the baking sheet.

Ask an adult to help you use the oven. Bake the granola at 325°F for 15 to 20 minutes, stirring gently after 10 minutes. When the granola is golden brown and slightly crispy, remove it from the oven. It will become crispier as it cools.

Stir in the dried fruit while the granola is still warm.

Cool completely, then store in an airtight container at room temperature for up to a week.

Serve the granola in a small bowl with milk or yogurt, or scoop up a handful for a quick snack on the go.

MAKES ABOUT 3 CUPS.

Next, Bear and Fox strolled over to Beaver's lodge in the stream. Bear pointed out where the wild mint grew and where he collected his honey.

"Greetings, Beaver! How was your winter?" called Bear.

"Magical!" said Beaver. "Mama Beaver and I have three brand-new baby kits."

"Congratulations! I'm so happy to meet them!" said Bear. "Fox is keen to sample some new foods. What have you been eating?"

"We've been gnawing on a lot of bark lately," said Beaver. "But I've been dreaming about sweet wild apples and the fresh watercress that grows along my stream."

Maple-Apple Crisp

Bear picks wild apples that grow at the edge of his forest and tosses them with syrup from maple trees to make this delicious dessert.

FILLING

4 cups peeled, cored and sliced apples (about 4 medium)*

2 tbsp maple syrup

2 tbsp brown sugar

½ to 1 tsp ground cinnamon (less for a milder taste)

TOPPING

½ cup rolled oats

¼ cup flour

½ cup brown sugar

¼ cup cold butter

Preheat the oven to 350°F.

Place the apple slices in a mixing bowl and add maple syrup, 2 tbsp sugar and the cinnamon. Toss the apple slices until they are lightly coated with the flavorings.

Place the apples in a buttered 9-inch pie plate.

To make the topping, mix together the oats, flour and ½ cup sugar in a bowl. With a pastry blender, cut in the cold butter until the mixture resembles coarse crumbs. (Or cut the butter into cubes and mix in with your fingers.)

Sprinkle the topping over the apples.

With an adult's help, bake at 350°F for about 45 minutes, or until the apples are tender and the topping is crispy and golden.

Serve warm, topped with a scoop of ice cream if desired.

Makes 6 servings.

*Any variety of apples will work in this dessert, but Bear's favorites are
 Ambrosia, Gala or McIntosh.

Deep in the forest, the two friends found Deer and
Hare nibbling on bright green herbs and leaves.

"We love the new plants of spring," said Deer.

"Try some," said Hare. "They are so tender at this time of year."

"I know just the recipe for them," said Bear.

Spring Greens Salad

Deer and Hare can hardly wait for the first greens of spring! Bear likes to serve this salad with a sweet and tart honey dressing.

SALAD

2 cups spring mix salad greens

1 cup "wild" greens*

12 to 16 cherry tomatoes, sliced in half

⅓ long English cucumber, diced

HONEY VINAIGRETTE

3 tbsp olive oil

1 tbsp apple cider vinegar

1½ tsp honey (warmed slightly — about 5 seconds in the microwave)

1 tsp Dijon mustard

salt and pepper to taste

with Honey Vinaigrette

Using a colander, rinse the greens and pat them dry with a clean towel or paper towel. Alternatively, you can use a salad spinner. Tear any large greens into smaller pieces, or remove the leaves from their stalks, as needed. Place all the greens in a bowl and gently toss them together.

Divide the greens between 4 side plates. Sprinkle them with sliced tomatoes and diced cucumber.

Combine the ingredients for the vinaigrette in a small jar. Screw the lid on tightly and shake the jar until the dressing is well blended.

With a teaspoon, trickle a small amount of dressing over each salad, then serve.

MAKES 4 SIDE SALADS.

OPTIONAL: To turn your salad into a heartier meal, top it with a handful of canned chickpeas, cooked chicken, fish, tofu, or grated or crumbled cheese.

*Many interesting greens grow in the spring and early summer. You might like to try one or more of the following: sorrel (for a lemony taste), arugula or watercress (for a peppery taste), mustard leaves (spicy!), dandelion (strong flavor), or fennel (for a licorice taste). You can experiment with different combinations to see which you like best.

Back at the den, Fox and Bear put on their aprons.
Fox said, "What's your favorite food, Bear?"
"I have a sweet tooth," said Bear. "I adore fruit desserts of any kind."
They chopped and sliced. Diced and stirred. Tossed and baked.
Poached and puréed. Simmered and sautéed. They cooked all
afternoon long.

Bear's Blueberry Muffins

Wild blueberries are one of Bear's favorite foods. He likes to eat them fresh or baked in these muffins.

2 cups flour

¾ cup sugar

1 tbsp baking powder

¼ tsp salt

2 eggs

1 cup milk

½ cup melted butter

grated rind of 1 lemon

1 cup blueberries (fresh or frozen)

Preheat the oven to 400°F.

Line a muffin tin with paper liners.

In a mixing bowl, stir together the flour, sugar, baking powder and salt.

In another bowl, whisk the eggs, then add the milk, melted butter and lemon rind and whisk until well mixed.

Add the wet ingredients to the dry ingredients, stirring until just blended. (Don't over-mix!) Gently stir in the blueberries.

Spoon the batter into the prepared muffin cups, dividing the batter equally between them.

With an adult's help, bake at 400°F for 15 to 20 minutes, or until the muffins are golden brown and a toothpick inserted comes out clean.

Cool slightly before serving.

MAKES 12 LARGE MUFFINS.

"It's time to taste," said Bear.
They had a nibble of each dish.
"Mmm . . ." said Fox. "I had no idea there was so much scrumptious food in the forest."
The two friends packed up everything.
"This should keep you going until more spring plants are in bloom," said Bear.

On the way back to Fox's burrow, they dropped off a nut burger for Squirrel, a bag of honey-roasted granola for Chickadee, a dish of maple-apple crisp for Beaver, mini blueberry muffins for the baby kits, and a spring greens salad for Deer and Hare.

Fox gave Bear a big hug.

"I'm going to practice for a while and then I will cook you dinner," said Fox.

"That will be wonderful!" said Bear.

As he ambled back to his den, Bear knew how he would pass the time until the spring sun had warmed up the forest, and it was wide awake and bustling with life once more.

He would write down all his recipes for Fox, so that his dear friend could enjoy many marvelous meals and never have to eat the same old thing again.

Watercress Tea Sandwiches

Beaver dreams of fresh watercress that grows in the spring. Bear serves him these dainty sandwiches with a cup of wild mint tea.

small handful of watercress

¼ cup softened cream cheese

2 slices of bread

8 (or more) thin cucumber slices (optional)

Rinse and pat dry a small bunch of watercress. Pick the leaves off the stems and discard the stems.

Spread cream cheese on each slice of bread.

Top the cream cheese with a sprinkle of watercress leaves (and thinly sliced cucumbers if desired).

Cut the sandwiches into quarters. Use a diagonal slice if you'd like to make triangle-shaped quarters. Arrange the sandwich pieces on a plate and serve.

MAKES 2 OPEN-FACED SANDWICHES.

OPTIONAL: Egg salad and watercress sandwiches are delicious, too. Simply spread egg salad mixture on slices of buttered bread and top with watercress leaves.

Wild Mint Tea

After a long, cold winter, Bear looks forward to the fresh taste of wild mint. He brews warm mugs of mint tea for his friends.

handful of fresh mint leaves
  (about ½ cup)

2 cups boiling water

spoonful of honey (optional)

Rinse the mint leaves and shake off the excess water. Remove the stems.

Tear the leaves into smaller pieces, then place them in a teapot with an inner strainer or a French press.*

Ask an adult to pour boiling water over the leaves. Let them steep for 3 to 7 minutes. The longer you steep them, the stronger the mint taste will be.

When the tea is ready, pour it into cups. Add a spoonful of honey to taste.

MAKES 2 CUPS.

* If you don't have either of these, simply pour the steeped tea through a strainer.

Blackberry-Raspberry Parfait

Sweet wild berries are a special treat for Bear. He makes this berry parfait for breakfast or as a midday snack.

1 cup blackberries*

1 cup raspberries*

2 cups Greek-style yogurt (plain or vanilla), or dairy-free yogurt

handful of granola (optional)

In a bowl, gently toss the blackberries and raspberries together.

Spoon a layer of yogurt into 4 small jelly jars, parfait glasses or individual glass bowls.

Next, add a layer of berries.

Top the berries with a layer of yogurt.

Repeat the layers.

Top with a layer of granola (see recipe on page 18), if desired. If you make your parfait in a jelly jar, you can screw on a lid and have a tasty lunch or snack to go. The parfait keeps well in the fridge overnight.

MAKES 4 SERVINGS.

*Bear says any combination of berries is delicious, including blueberries and sliced strawberries. Mix and match berries to make your favorite parfait!

Wild Strawberry Smoothie

Bear is very fond of wild strawberries, but any kind of berry or combination of berries would be yummy in this smoothie. Chickadee agrees!

1 cup strawberries, fresh or frozen	⅓ cup milk *
1 banana	1 tbsp honey
½ cup vanilla yogurt *	2 or 3 ice cubes

Ask an adult to help you use the blender. Place all the ingredients in the blender and put a lid on it.

Purée the ingredients until they are smooth. Pour into glasses.

MAKES ABOUT 2 CUPS.

*To make a nondairy smoothie, you can substitute dairy-free yogurt or soft tofu for the yogurt, and soy or almond milk for the milk.

crunchy Apple Salad

Beaver loves the crunch of this fresh apple salad. Bear hopes you like it, too.

1 large apple, cored and chopped
   into bite-sized pieces

⅓ cup diced celery (about 1 stalk)

½ cup red seedless grapes, sliced
   in half

HONEY-YOGURT DRESSING

¼ cup plain Greek-style yogurt

1 tbsp honey (warmed slightly —
   about 5 seconds in the microwave)

½ tsp lemon juice

In a medium-sized bowl, toss together the apple, celery and grapes.

In a small bowl, mix together the yogurt, honey and lemon juice.

Pour the dressing over the salad mixture and toss until well coated. Serve immediately in small bowls or on side plates.

MAKES 4 SMALL SERVINGS OR
2 LARGER ONES.

Honey-Cinnamon Applesauce

Bear knows that apples become soft and sweet when they are cooked. He eats his applesauce with a drizzle of honey and a sprinkle of cinnamon.

4 medium apples, peeled, cored
and roughly chopped

½ cup water

pinch of cinnamon (optional)

spoonful of honey (optional)

Ask an adult for help with the stove. Place the apples in a saucepan with the water over high heat and bring to a boil. Then turn down the heat, and cover and simmer on low to medium heat until the apples are very tender (about 20 minutes).

Remove from heat. Using a potato masher or fork (being careful to avoid splashing), mash the apples until they are as smooth as you like them.

Once the applesauce has cooled slightly, taste it to see if you'd like to stir in a little cinnamon or honey. Depending on how sweet your apples are, you may or may not need it.

You can eat your applesauce warm or cold. It will keep in the fridge for 3 or 4 days.

MAKES ABOUT 2 CUPS.

Wild Onion and Cheddar Egg Tarts

Bear picks wild onions in his forest, but you can use fresh chives in this recipe. If you're not keen on an onion taste, simply leave out the chives.

1 cup grated aged cheddar cheese

6 large eggs

½ cup milk

a pinch or two each of salt and pepper

2 tsp finely chopped fresh chives

Preheat the oven to 350°F.

Line a muffin tin with paper liners.

Divide the grated cheese among the muffin cups.

In a mixing bowl, whisk together the eggs and milk until they are one color. Stir in the salt and pepper.

Transfer the egg mixture into a large measuring cup with a spout.

Pour an equal amount of egg mixture into each muffin cup so they are about a third full. Sprinkle the tops with chopped chives.

With an adult's help, bake the egg tarts at 350°F for 15 to 20 minutes, until they puff up and are just set, or until a toothpick inserted into them comes out clean.

Cool slightly before pulling away the paper liners. The egg tarts may be eaten warm or stored in the fridge and eaten cold. (A cold tart can also be warmed in the microwave for 15 to 20 seconds.)

MAKES 12 TARTS.

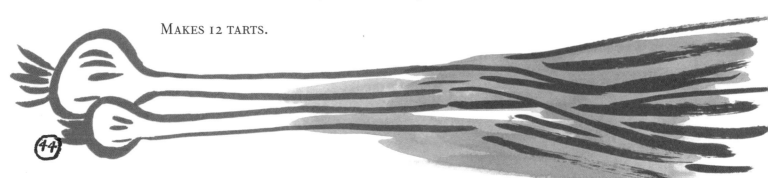

Wild Greens Pita Pizza

Bear likes the peppery taste of wild arugula on his pizza, but you can try other greens, too.

2 Greek-style pitas (or any similar-sized flatbread)

¼ cup pizza sauce

large handful of baby arugula

sliced mushrooms, chopped peppers or other pizza toppings (optional)

⅔ cup grated mozzarella cheese (or more to taste)

Preheat the oven to 425°F.

Place the pitas on a baking sheet. With the back of a spoon, spread the sauce evenly over the pitas.

Top with a handful of baby arugula or other greens (sorrel, mustard, fennel, basil, oregano and so on) and any other pizza toppings you'd like, such as mushrooms or peppers.

Sprinkle on the cheese.

With an adult's help, bake at 425°F for 8 to 10 minutes, or until the cheese is bubbling and lightly browned.

Cool slightly, then transfer the pizzas to a cutting board. Cut the pizzas into quarters and serve.

MAKES 2 INDIVIDUAL-SIZED PIZZAS.

Hazelnut-Chocolate Chip Cookies

Bear thanks Squirrel for sharing her hazelnuts. He knows she'll love these fudgy, nutty cookies.

½ cup butter, softened

½ cup brown sugar

¼ cup white sugar

1 egg

¾ tsp vanilla

1 cup and 2 tbsp flour

½ tsp baking soda

¼ tsp salt

1 cup semi-sweet chocolate chips

½ cup hazelnuts, coarsely ground*

Preheat the oven to 375°F.

In a mixing bowl, using a wooden spoon or hand mixer, cream together the butter and sugars.

Add the egg and vanilla and beat or stir until well blended.

In another bowl, mix together the flour, baking soda and salt.

Add the flour mixture to the creamed mixture and stir until it is well combined.

Mix in the chocolate chips and hazelnuts.

Drop rounded 1 tbsp portions of dough, 1 inch apart, onto an ungreased cookie sheet. (For easier clean-up, use a cookie sheet lined with parchment paper.)

With an adult's help, bake at 375°F for 8 to 10 minutes, or until the cookies are golden brown.

Cool slightly, then enjoy!

MAKES ABOUT 2 DOZEN.

*Ask an adult to help you grind the nuts in a blender or food processor, pulsing them for a few seconds at a time until they are a coarse grind. (You can substitute other nuts, such as walnuts or pecans, if you prefer. And if you like nut-free cookies, simply leave out the nuts.)

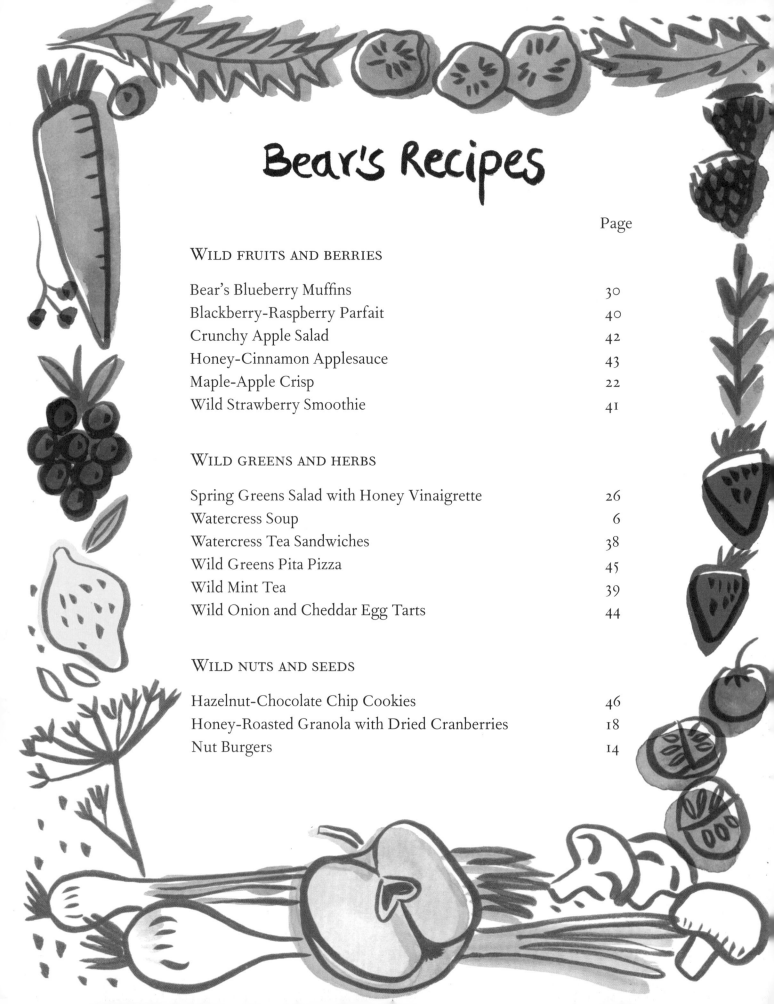

Bear's Recipes